Bunkie and the Ugly Shirt

DONALD HASLETT JR.

Illustrated By Mark Ruben Abacajan

Copyright © 2015 by Donald Haslett Jr. 722131
ISBN: Softcover   978-1-5035-9578-1
        EBook   978-1-5035-9579-8

All rights reserved. No part of this book may be reproduced or transmitted in any form or by any means, electronic or mechanical, including photocopying, recording, or by any information storage and retrieval system, without permission in writing from the copyright owner.

This is a work of fiction. Names, characters, places and incidents either are the product of the author's imagination or are used fictitiously, and any resemblance to any actual persons, living or dead, events, or locales is entirely coincidental.

Print information available on the last page

Rev. date: 09/01/2015

To order additional copies of this book, contact:
Xlibris
1-888-795-4274
www.Xlibris.com
Orders@Xlibris.com

Bunkie
and the
Ugly Shirt

DONALD HASLETT JR.

Officer Bunkie was proud to be a part of an elite security force at the Nevada Gold Mining Company. Bunkie had spent hours shining his steel toe boots. He had polished his badge so fine that it would shine for miles in the sun. Bunkie wore a black tie with his cross pistols tie tack. The cross pistols were a symbol of the military police. He had served 8 years in the Army Reserves as a military police officer.

Bunkie was a member of the FPA or the Fun Police Association. A fellow officer asked Bunkie if we had to arrest people for having too much fun. Bunkie replied that, "the FPA was dedicated to making security officers more professional." Bunkie further added, "we don't want to arrest persons for having fun, but encourage it as long as it does not harm others."

Officer Bunkie noticed from the work schedule that he would be off the next day. Bunkie made a plan to go shopping for some much needed socks and underwear. Bunkie's favorite store of choice was Clothes Unlimited.

As Bunkie patrolled the men's clothing department at Clothes Unlimited he observed a dress shirt sale. Now Bunkie always had a fascination for dress shirts. After investigating the shirts he came to an ugly shirt on the bottom of the pile. Bunkie thought to himself, "who would buy such an ugly shirt?" Bunkie spoke out loud and said, "I wouldn't be caught dead wearing this ugly shirt." A pretty young sales clerk chuckled at Bunkie's remarks.

Upon examination of the ugly shirt, Bunkie discovered it was his exact size. Upon further inspection of the shirt, Bunkie found that the shirt had been reduced in price, not once, not twice, but five times. Five times the original price of $47.00. The shirt only cost $4.00 now. Bunkie never owned an ugly shirt before and didn't know what consequences it would bring.

Well Bunkie said to himself, there's always a first time for everything. So since the ugly shirt had the perfect Bunkie fit and had the perfect Bunkie price, he became the proud owner of an ugly shirt.

Almost immediately, Bunkie was extremely excited about bringing his newly purchased shirt home. You would have thought he was bringing home a new born baby. Bunkie wondered if Clothes Unlimited would ever recover their financial loss from selling this shirt at such a low price. Bunkie praised himself as the master of all bargain hunters. Bunkie couldn't wait to take his shirt into work and have his security buddies guess at how much he paid. After all $4.00 should give Bunkie bragging rights too.

In his excitement Bunkie decided to dance with his shirt. After about a minute of the Bunkie Rock, he remembered, "Holy Cow, I forgot to get socks and underwear."

Days following Bunkie's purchase became anything but normal. Bunkie met stiff resistance and discrimination everywhere he wore his ugly shirt. Even his wife of 20 years, told Bunkie, "get rid of that shirt or I am leaving you." Bunkie explained to his wife that Clothes Unlimited had a very strict no return policy. Bunkie further added that Clothes Unlimited enforced this policy with guards stationed at all entrances armed with automatic weapons.

Bunkie's wife did not care and left him anyway. She packed her bags and left with a shirtless man from Fun Land. Bunkie had no use for shirtless men. Bunkie's motto was no shirt, no character.

Bunkie's problems did not end there. The Lucky 7 Casino sent Bunkie a certified letter informing him he would no longer get free drinks, free food, and free slot machine play. They informed him that anybody with a bad taste in clothing should not get free stuff.

Bunkie's only salvation was a sweet woman from the Motor City. Her name was Spunkie and he had dated her years ago before he was married. Recently he had found out she was still single after all these years.

Bunkie went back to work to forget about all the troubles this shirt caused him. He was patrolling the mine site during day watch when he noticed a dark cloud of smoke. Bunkie immediately responded to the dark cloud of smoke and realized that the mine was on fire. Bunkie saw the mine rescue team working to get the miners out safely. Bunkie had great respect for the mine rescue team. These guys were all miners and volunteers risking their own life to save others. They were trained in firefighting and first aid. On several occasions Bunkie had assisted the mine rescue team with first aid and transporting injured miners to the hospital.

Bunkie met the mine rescue team captain and volunteered his assistance. The captain stated that the fire had been extinguished and all the miners had been successfully pulled out of the mine. The captain went on to say that the medical helicopters or medivac are not familiar with this new gold mine and it could be a while for them to find us. Several miners needed immediate medical attention or they could die. The captain wondered if Bunkie could figure a way to direct the helicopters to the location of the badly burned miners.

Bunkie remembered that the miners being a very patriotic bunch of guys had put up a rather tall flag pole. Bunkie took the ugly shirt from his bag and tied it to the flag ropes. He raised the ugly shirt like you would a flag. He then radioed the Medivac copters to look for the ugly shirt in the sky. He told them to look for the ugly shirt and that's where you want to land.

Bunkie became a celebrity overnight with his fast thinking that saved the miners. He was a celebrity locally in his community and nationally as well. The Lucky 7 Casino reinstated Bunkie's free compensation with free drinks, free food, and free spending money. In fact, the Lucky 7 Casino told Bunkie he could eat for free in their buffet all month.

The mayor hearing about Bunkie's heroic deed invited him to city hall to receive the key to the city. Bunkie asked Miss Spunkie to be at his side to receive this award. He ask Miss Spunkie to be at his side, not as his girlfriend, but as his future wife. She accepted and they drove to city hall.

Bunkie gladly accepted the golden key to the city. Bunkie recited these words. "Just as we should never judge a book by its cover, we should also never judge an ugly shirt by its looks." And Bunkie went on to say," For the beauty in one ugly shirt that day came from saving lives."

Edwards Brothers Malloy
Oxnard, CA USA
September 11, 2015